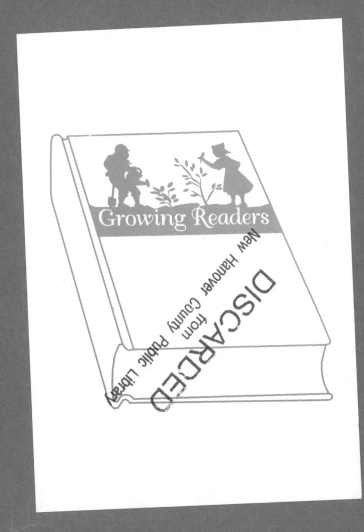

FOLLOW ME!

BY BETHANY ROBERTS ILLUSTRATED BY DIANE GREENSEID

CLARION BOOKS/NEW YORK

Clarion Books
a Houghton Mifflin Company imprint
215 Park Avenue South, New York, NY 10003
Text copyright © 1998 by Bethany Roberts
Illustrations copyright © 1998 by Diane Greenseid

Type is set in 16/21-point Bookman demi.
The illustrations for this book are executed in acrylics on watercolor paper.

Printed in the U.S.A..

Library of Congress Cataloging-in-Publication Data

Roberts, Bethany.
Follow me! / by Bethany Roberts ; illustrated by Diane Greenseid.
p.   cm.
Summary: A mother octopus leads her little ones past all sorts of sea creatures
as they make their way through the underwater world.
ISBN 0-395-82268-8
[1. Octopus—Fiction. 2. Marine animals—Fiction. 3. Stories in rhyme.]
I. Greenseid, Diane, ill. II. Title.
PZ8.3.R5295Fo   1998
[E]—dc21   97-48304
AC

HOR 10 9 8 7 6 5 4 3 2 1

To Krista, with love
—B.R.

For Melinda, with love
—D.G.

"Come," said Octopus Mum
to her eight little octopuses
all in a row, "let's leave our cozy cave
and go.

Swim over here where clown fish play
beneath this ledge—I'll lead the way."

"Where are we going?"
"Wait and see, my little ones,
just follow me.

Wave to the crabs,
glide through these weeds.

Say hi to turtles in the reeds.

**Blow bubbles
with this parrot fish.**

**Dance with shrimp
where grasses swish.**

**Sing with clams
in sandy homes.**

With jellyfish
float on the foam.

With angelfish
play hide-and-seek,

in holes and cracks
we'll search and peek.

Let's swim where purple sea fans sway,
gardens bloom, and starfish play.

Tiptoe past this coral reef . . .

LOOK OUT!

An eel with pointy teeth!

**Hurry!
Squirt a cloud of ink!**

20

Now
down
we
sink.

Around this bend—

swim faster.
Soar!

23

Then zoom down to the ocean floor.

We're almost there.

A zag! A zip!

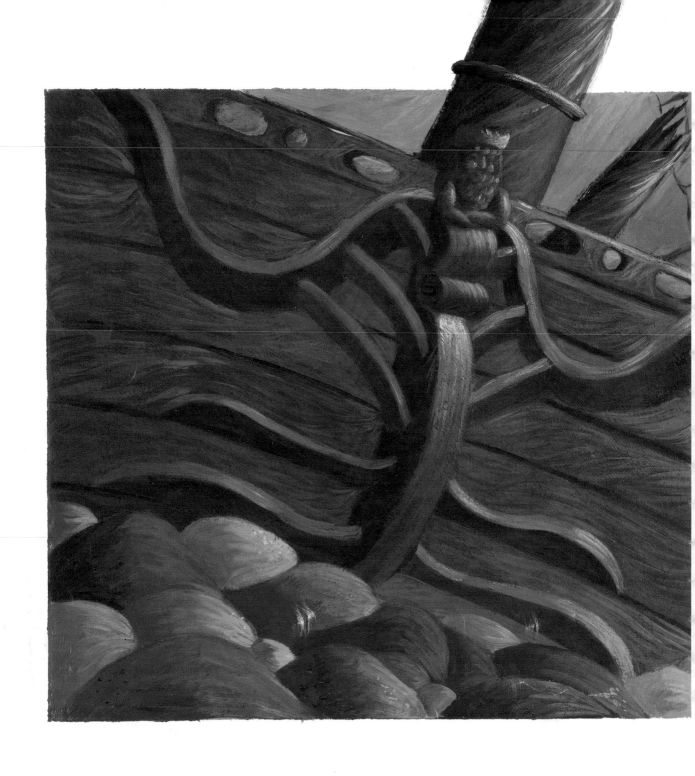

Now whiz inside this pirate ship.

Safe at last.

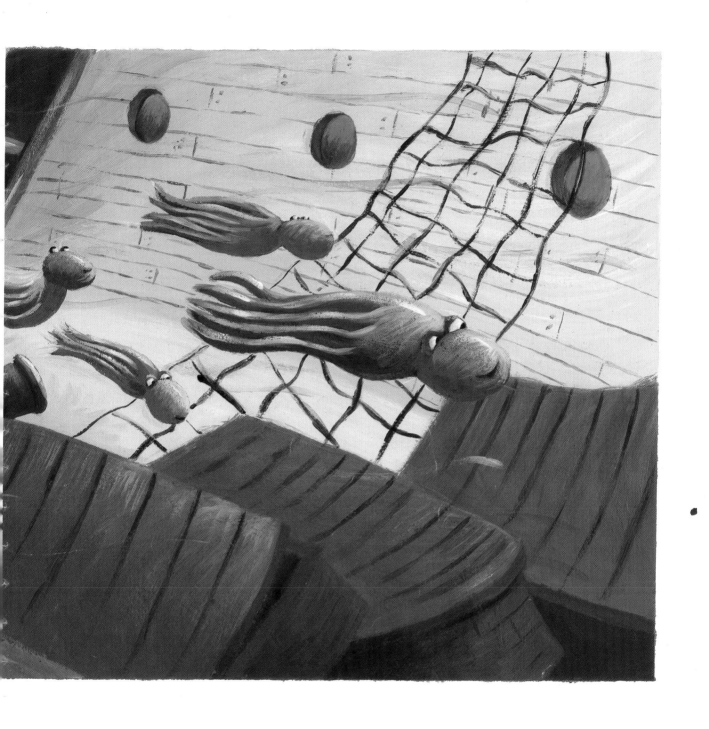

And look!
Behind this wall . . .

is Grandma with a hug for all.